Rotten and Rascal

The Two Terrible Pterosaur Twins

Paul Geraghty

ANDERSEN PRESS

Rotten
and Rascal

For Mrs Marvellous

Also by Paul Geraghty:

Dinosaur in Danger

Help Me!

The Hunter

Slobcat

Solo

Tortuga

This paperback edition first published in 2013 by Andersen Press Ltd.
20 Vauxhall Bridge Road, London SW1V 2SA.
First published in Great Britain in 2006 by Hutchinson.
Published in Australia by Random House Australia Pty.,
Level 3, 100 Pacific Highway, North Sydney, NSW 2060.
Copyright © Paul Geraghty, 2006.
The rights of Paul Geraghty to be identified as the author and illustrator
of this work have been asserted by him in accordance with the Copyright,
Designs and Patents Act, 1988.
All rights reserved.
Printed and bound in Singapore by Tien Wah Press.

10   9   8   7   6   5   4   3   2

British Library Cataloguing in Publication Data available.

ISBN 978 1 84939 563 2

65 million years ago the world was a deafening place.

There were thunderstorms.

There were volcanoes.

There were landslides.

And there were earthquakes.

But most of the noise came from
Rotten and **Rascal,**
two terrible pterosaur twins.
By day they would yell at each other,
by night they would shout.

Come morning they'd be *screeching,*
by lunch they'd be **screaming** and
before bed they'd be **bellowing** again.

They just never stopped.

On Tuesday, Rotten saw a fish.

"It's **mine!**" yelled Rascal and they both dived down.

"I saw it **first!**" shouted Rotten.

"I saw it **loudest!**" bellowed Rascal.

And there was a hullabaloo . . .

. . . until Slim sidled up and said, "You gotta have a good beak, brother. The fish should go to the one with the best beak."

"No it's not," shrieked Rotten. "The fish is mine!"

"It's mine!" "It's mine!"

And there was a horrible hullabaloo . . .

. . . until Violet veered into view and said, "Hey, man, cool down. The fish should go to the one with the best crest."

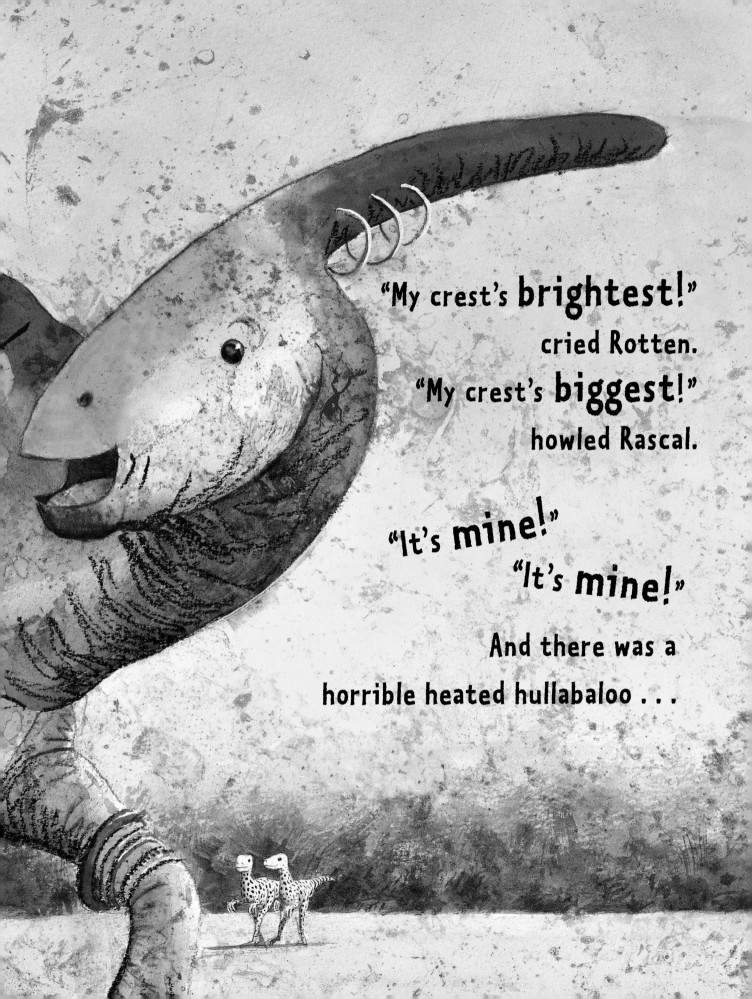

"My crest's **brightest!**"
cried Rotten.
"My crest's **biggest!**"
howled Rascal.

"It's **mine!**"
"It's **mine!**"

And there was a
horrible heated hullabaloo . . .

. . . until Slippery swam up and said,
"It's simple: the best swimmer should get the fish."
"I swim fastest!" shouted Rotten.
"I dive deepest!" shrieked Rascal.
"No you don't!" screamed Rotten. "The fish is **mine!**"

"It's mine!"
"It's mine!"

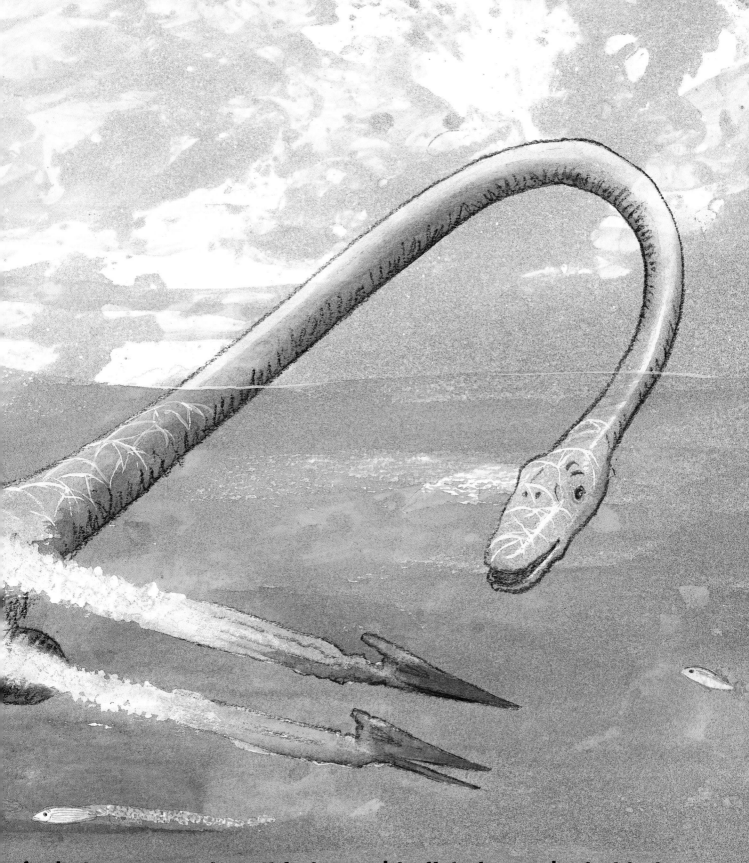

And there was a horrible heated hullabaloo and a hubbub . . .

. . . until Clever concocted a cunning conclusion.

"The fish should go to the one who argues the least."

"I argue **less**," claimed Rotten.

"I argue the **least**," argued Rascal.

"No you don't," screamed Rotten. "The fish is **mine!**"

"It's **mine!**"   "It's **mine!**"

And there was a horrible heated
hullabaloo and a howling hubbub . . .

... until Buster burst in and bellowed, "What's the problem? The fish should go to the toughest pterosaur."

"I'm **toughest!**" yelled Rotten.
"Can't be," howled Rascal,
"'cause I'm **tougher!**"

"Oh yeah?"
"Try me!"

So they kicked and fought till they both fell
to the floor, too tired to talk.

For a wonderful moment there was silence.

"I won," Rotten panted at last.
"I won," huffed Rascal.
"No you didn't. I won!"
"No you didn't. I won!"
And there was a horrible hysterical heated
hullabaloo and a howling hubbub . . .

. . . until Rex roared, "**HEY!** Cut the scrapping and yelling. Which one of you is the **fattest**, the **juiciest**, the **crunchiest** and the **tastiest?**"

"I'm **fattest!**" yelled Rotten.

"I'm **juiciest!**" shouted Rascal.

"I'm the **crunchiest!**" bellowed Rotten.

"I'm the **tastiest!**" screamed Rascal . . .

. . . then they saw the gleam in Rex's eye.

Two terrified pterosaur twins tongue-tied in a
tyrannosaurus-shaped shadow finally stopped fighting.

But it was too late . . .

And just in case you were wondering,
they both tasted exactly the same.